THE LIBRARY

THE Library

SARAH STEWART

Pictures by

DAVID SMALL

SQUARE
FISH

Farrar Straus Giroux
New York

To the memory of the real
Mary Elizabeth Brown
Librarian, Reader, Friend
1920 – 1991

SQUARE
FISH

An Imprint of Macmillan

THE LIBRARY. Text copyright © 1995 by Sarah Stewart. Pictures copyright © 1995 by David Small.
All rights reserved. Printed in China by South China Printing Company Ltd.,
Dongguan City, Guangdong Province. For information, address
Square Fish, 175 Fifth Avenue, New York, NY 10010.

Square Fish and the Square Fish logo are trademarks of Macmillan
and are used by Farrar Straus Giroux under license from Macmillan.

Library of Congress Cataloging-in-Publication Data
Stewart, Sarah.
The library / Sarah Stewart ; pictures by David Small.
p. cm.
Summary: Elizabeth Brown loves to read more than anything else, but when her
collection of books grows and grows, she must make a change in her life.
ISBN 978-0-312-38454-8
[1. Books and reading—Fiction. 2. Stories in rhyme.] I. Small, David, 1945- ill. II. Title.
PZ8.3.S855Li   1995
[E]—dc20   94-30320

Originally published in the United States by Farrar Straus Giroux
Square Fish logo designed by Filomena Tuosto
First Square Fish Edition: September 2008
5 7 9 10 8 6 4
mackids.com

AR: 3.3 / LEXILE: NP

Elizabeth Brown
Entered the world
Dropping straight down from the sky.

Elizabeth Brown
Entered the world
Skinny, nearsighted, and shy.

She didn't like to play with dolls,
She didn't like to skate.
She learned to read quite early
And at an incredible rate.

 She always took a book to bed,
With a flashlight under the sheet.
She'd make a tent of covers
And read herself to sleep.

Elizabeth Brown
Went off to school
Dragging a steamer trunk.

 Elizabeth Brown
Unpacked her books,
Breaking the upper bunk.

 She sat in all her classes
And doodled on a pad,
Adrift in dreams of entering
A readers' olympiad.

 She manufactured library cards
And checked out books to friends,
Then shocked them with her midnight raids
To collect the books again.

Elizabeth Brown
Preferred a book
To going on a date.

While friends went out
And danced till dawn,
She stayed up reading late.

She took the train one afternoon
And promptly lost her way,
So bought a house and settled down
To tutoring for pay.

Elizabeth Brown
Walked into town
Summer, fall, winter, and spring.

Elizabeth Brown
Walked into town
Looking for only one thing.

She didn't want potato chips,
She didn't want new clothes.
She went straight to the bookstore.
"May I have one of **those**?"

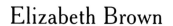

Elizabeth Brown
Walked right back home
And read and read and read.

She even read while
Exercising,
And standing on her head.

 She made a list of groceries
And tucked it in her book,
Then lost the list among the fruits
And left with nothing to cook.

She read about Greek goddesses
While vacuuming the floor.
Attending only to her book,
She'd walk into a door.

Books were piled on top of chairs
And spread across the floor.
Her shelves began to fall apart,
As she read more and more.

Big books made very solid stacks
On which teacups could rest.
Small books became the building blocks
For busy little guests.

When volumes climbed the parlor walls
And blocked the big front door,
She had to face the awful fact
She could not have one more.

Elizabeth Brown
Walked into town
That very afternoon.

Elizabeth Brown
Walked into town
Whistling a happy tune.

She didn't want a bicycle,
She didn't want silk bows.
She went straight to the courthouse—
"May I have one of **those**?"

The form was for donations.
She quickly wrote this line:
"I, E. Brown, give to the town
All that was ever mine."

Elizabeth Brown
Moved in with a friend
And lived to a ripe old age.

They walked to the library
Day after day,
And turned page...
after page...

after page.

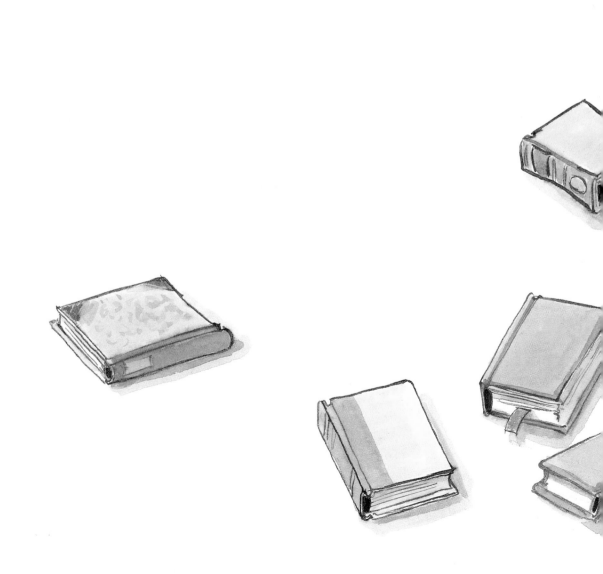